The Durples

Get Lost in Elkton Forest

by

Kathy Jardine & Ashley Jardine

AuthorHouse™
1663 Liberty Drive, Suite 200
Bloomington, IN 47403
www.authorhouse.com
Phone: 1-800-839-8640

First published by AuthorHouse 10/3/2007

ISBN: 978-1-4343-1317-1 (sc)

Library of Congress Control Number: 2007905148

Printed in the United States of America
Bloomington, Indiana

This book is printed on acid-free paper.

authorHOUSE®

"Treat everyone with kindness, even those who are not kind to you - not because they are nice, but because you are."

~Author Unknown

Mollyboo, Cindyloo, and Woodroo walked along the trail toward home, taking turns kicking a ball and talking. Cindyloo was the youngest of them and wore a black-and

ite checkered hat. Mollyboo's favorite color was blue, so
e wore a blue hat and a blue scarf to go with her blue
ir. Woodroo was the oldest brother of the three and
e biggest. His favorite color was also blue and he wore
blue hat and a blue scarf too. It was a sunny day and
e Durples walked for hours. They were so deep in their
nversation they forgot to make their turn at the big oak
ee.

the time they realized where they were, it was too late,
d they were lost in Elkton Forest.

Vho-who is going to find us?" cried Cindyloo.
Ve will be all right," comforted Mollyboo.
Vould you hold my hand?" cried Woodroo. "Would you?"
erhaps we will all hold hands," said Mollyboo as she
ched onto the hands of her brother and sister.

"Who, who, who," they heard off in the distance.
"Who-who is there?" yelled Cindyloo.

"It's an owl and they say who-who just like you," laughed Mollyboo.

"Would you say we are lost, Mollyboo? Would you? I would," said Woodroo.

"I'm sure we will find our way back home," said Mollyboo.

"Look, someone lives over there," pointed out Mollyboo.

"We'll go over and ask if they can help us."

Just short of the cabin door, they stopped. It was so quiet they could hear the wind blowing through the trees in a song of sadness.

Did they dare knock on the door?

Knock. Knock. Knock.

The door opened, and there stood a big, tall, unsightly, hunchbacked creature.

They screamed, "Eeeeeeek!"

The Creature screamed, "Ahhhhh!"

The trio stood there, paralyzed with fear.

The Durples were in desperate need of help finding their way home. Cindyloo piped up, "Who-who are you?" in a trembling, high-pitched voice.

"I'm Odalee McBuddy," he said shyly, looking down to the ground. "And who are you?"

"We're the Durples. I'm Mollyboo. This is my sister Cindyloo and my brother Woodroo, and we're lost here in the forest."

"Would you help us find the way home? Would you?" asked Woodroo.

"Oh ... You're lost. That would explain why you're here." He sighed. "I never get visitors. People always throw rocks at me, or just run away."

Mollyboo could sense Odalee's sadness. "That's mean! We would never throw rocks at you. This is the only house we could see for miles and we knocked on your door so that you could hopefully help us find our way home to Turpleville."

"So, Odalee, would you know how to get to Turpleville? Would you?" asked Woodroo.

"Oh, that's pretty far. I was just fixing up a sandwich. It would be good to have a full stomach for the journey. You must be hungry. I will make you a snack and we will set out for Turpleville."

The Durples looked at each other, and all at the same time their hungry little bellies rumbled.

dalee fixed them a snack of sandwiches and milk. As
they ate hungrily, he told them the story of how he ended
up living in the middle of Elkton Forest. He was forced out
of his home because he was "different" and therefore he
built a quiet cabin to live alone in the forest. The Durples
were saddened by the thought of this nice creature being
treated badly, and they assured him that it is what is on
the inside that counts and that he was very kind.

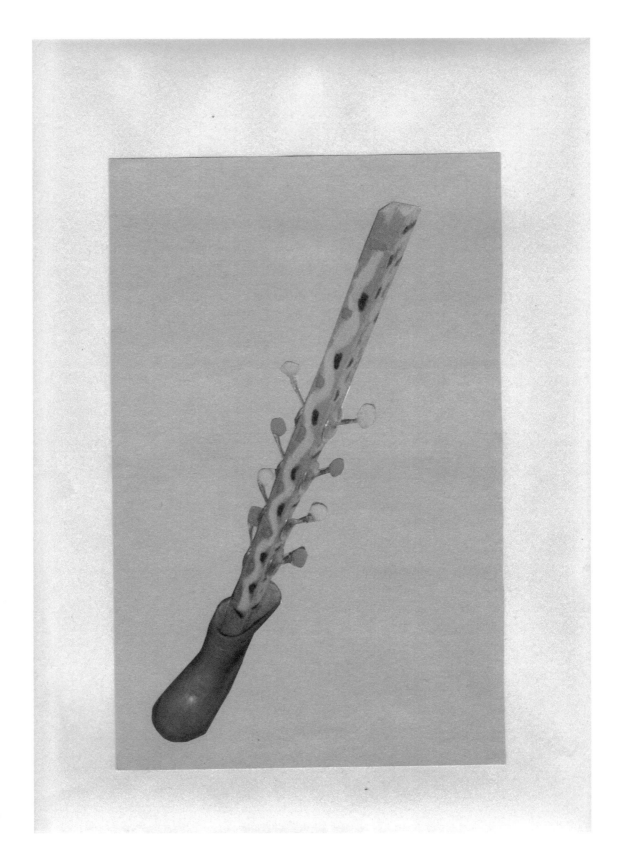

It was then that Odalee introduced the Durples to his mookaluke.

"It's my musical instrument that I made." He brought out a weird-looking boot attached to a stick with noisy things hanging off it, but it sure made nice music. "You play it by thumping it up and down on the ground. Absolutely anyone can play it!"

"Would you let me play it? Would you? I would," said Woodroo.

"Of course," replied Odalee. "You can all take turns."

"Sing us a song!" exclaimed Mollyboo.

He thumped the mookaluke on the floor and in rhythm he sang:

et's play the mookaluke,
et's play the mookaluke,
et's play the mookaluke, one, two, three.
Jon't someone come sing with me?
m just looking for friends, you see.
et's play the mookaluke,
et's play the mookaluke,
et's play the mookaluke, one, two, three.
on't judge me on what you see,
ause I'm just nice and friendly.

hey all took turns playing the mookaluke, singing and
ughing together. They were having so much fun that they
most forgot they were lost.

"We must not stay here anymore; we have a long journey ahead of us," explained Odalee, packing up his mookaluke. With full bellies and a new friend, the Durples set off into the forest on their way to Turpleville.

They walked about a mile or so down the path when they heard a rustling sound behind a tree. "Who-who is there?" asked Cindyloo.

All they could *see* was a fur ball rolling around. Then out jumped a scruffy little white dog with glasses and a gold tooth, and with an accent he said,
"Hello, mates! My name is Willy, Willy Wagstail."

"Hello to you too," replied Mollyboo. "We're the Durples. I'm Mollyboo, this is my sister Cindyloo, my brother Woodroo, and last but not least, our new friend Odalee McBuddy. What are you doing out here in the forest?"

"Actually I am lost. I was on my way to Turpleville and all of a sudden a gust of wind came up and leaves were blowing. My glasses got all fogged up and I must have taken a wrong turn. It's the strangest thing. I've never been lost before."

"We are from Turpleville! And we are lost too!" exclaimed Mollyboo. "Odalee is showing us the way home."

"We must keep moving," insisted Odalee.

"What's that neat looking thing you're carrying?" Willy asked Odalee curiously.

"It's my mookaluke. I will show you how it works later, but now we must be on our way."

Then there were five and they were on their way.

Suddenly the path they were walking down became very narrow, and when they rounded the bend, there was a big locked iron gate in their way.

"Who-who is going to open the gate?" asked Cindyloo. "What are we going to do now?"

At that moment a grumpy little green-and-yellow creature popped out from behind the gate.

"I know what you are!" exclaimed Willy. "You're one of those Bullions."

"Yes, I am. What's it to you?" snarled the Bullion. "My name is Billy and I guard this gate."

"Would you open the gate, please? Would you? I would," said Woodroo.

"Absolutely not. I've been told, no matter who you are, no one gets through this gate without a piece of gold."

"Gold? We don't have any gold. Who-who made up this rule?" asked Cindyloo.

"That would be my boss, AJ, and you do not want to make him mad," replied Billy. "He is King of the forest, you know."

"But-but, nobody owns this forest," argued Mollyboo.

"I don't care what you all say!" yelled Billy. "No one gets through this gate without a piece of gold!"

"Don't be silly, Billy. We don't have any gold."

"Then be off with you and don't come back until you have some gold to pay the toll."

Mollyboo asked, "Why are you such a bully, Billy?"

"It's my job," grunted Billy.

"Who-who would want a job being a bully?" asked Cindyloo.

"I have no family or friends, and this is the only work I can find. Now go and leave me alone," muttered Billy.

The five travelers stood in disbelief, trying to think of what to do. Odalee suggested walking back to the clearing they had passed and resting while trying to figure out where to get gold. They found the clearing and sat on the grass, wondering what to do next. Odalee brought out his mookaluke and they all started singing.

Let's play the mookaluke,
Let's play the mookaluke,
Let's play the mookaluke, one, two, three.
We are looking for gold you see.
Let's play the mookaluke,
Let's play the mookaluke,
Let's play the mookaluke, one, two, three.
We need gold in order to pay,
To get through the gate and we'll be on our way.
All of a sudden Willy jumped up and down, yelling, "I got it, I got it!"
"What?" asked Mollyboo.
"I have gold!"
"Where did you get gold?" asked Mollyboo.
"My tooth is gold," exclaimed Willy.
"You would give up your gold tooth for us?" asked Odalee.

"Of course I would!" replied Willy.

"Awwww, you are a true friend!" said Mollyboo.

Meanwhile Billy could hear them singing and talking and heard what Willy was going to do for his friends. Right then he decided he did not want to do this job anymore. He wanted to feel what these people felt: what it was like to have a true friend.

They all proudly walked up to the gate.

"We have a piece of gold; will you let us through now, please?" asked Willy.

"I will not take your gold, but I will let you through the gate as long as I can come with you to start a new life in Purpleville. I'm sorry for being such a bully. I don't want this job anymore. I'm so lonely, and when I heard Willy would give up his gold tooth for his friends, that changed my mind," explained Billy. "I've never had a friend before."

With sad eyes that glimmered with hope and admiration, Billy waited for an answer. The Durples, Odalee, and Willy exchanged glances.

"Sure, you can come with us," said Mollyboo. "The more the merrier. But I must warn you, bullies are not allowed in Turpleville, so you can never be a bully again if you come with us."

"Of course," said Billy excitedly. "I promise to never bully again."

Mollyboo could tell that Billy was sincere and reached out her hand to shake his. "We're the Durples. I'm Mollyboo. This is my sister Cindyloo, my brother Woodroo, our friends Odalee McBuddy and Willy Wagstail, and we are trying to get to Turpleville. Do you know which way to go?"

"Yes, you are definitely headed in the right direction," said Billy. "We must be on our way before my boss finds out what I have done."

hen there were six and they were on their way.

They walked along for hours, talking and laughing, with no promise of Turpleville in sight. Billy the Bullion hadn't been this happy in years. All of a sudden, they could hear cries coming from far away. The curious group of friends followed the cries until they found a girl standing under a big tree, crying. They crept up closer to the girl and she must have heard them coming. She turned around and yelled, "Don't laugh at me! Just keep going on your way!" She covered her face and began to cry harder.

"Who-who is going to laugh at you?" asked Cindyloo.

"Everyone laughs at me because I have to wear a brace on my leg, and I walk different," she said between sobs. "Just go away!"

"We would never laugh at you," comforted Mollyboo in a soft voice. "As I've told my friends here before, we come from a place called Turpleville, and in Turpleville we like unique people. It makes someone special to be different; special in their own way."

"You're from Turpleville?" she asked, wiping the tears from her big green eyes. "My grandma lives there and I was just on my way to pay her a visit. She always makes me feel better, and she bakes the best cookies in town."

"So would you know the way from here? Would you?" asked Woodroo.

"Of course. You are very close; it's just over the hill past the big oak tree. If that's where you are headed, I could show you the way," suggested the girl, looking down shyly at her leg brace. "I'm Princess Lilly."

"Wow, are you a real princess?" asked wide-eyed Willy.

"Yes, my mom is Queen of the Flowers of the Forest. Sh was born with special powers which bring spring flowers."

"Wow!" They all gasped.

"We're the Durples. I'm Mollyboo. This is my sister Cindyloo and my brother Woodroo, and our new friends Odalee, Willy, and Billy. We are honored to meet you, Princess Lilly."

"I would walk with you to Turpleville," Woodroo answered Princess Lilly. "Would you?" he asked the rest. "I would," said Woodroo, nodding his head in acceptance of the princess.

Princess Lilly smiled happily. They all agreed that they would love to have Princess Lilly in their company while walking the rest of the way to the promises of Turpleville. "What is that?" asked Princess Lilly, pointing at the odd-shaped instrument Odalee had in his hands.

"It's my mookaluke," he answered. "We will all play it later, but we must be going now."

Now there were seven and they were on their way.

They walked and talked, and as they got to know each other, the Durples soon realized that their new friends had something in common. Each of them shared stories of being bullied. They had been made fun of for the way they talked or walked or looked. Mollyboo was quick to reassure them that it is what is on the inside that counts. Mollyboo, Cindyloo, and Woodroo were thankful that they grew up in a place where everybody was treated with kindness and bullying was unheard of. It gave the Durples the good fortune to meet their new friends and give them all something they'd never had: true friends who cared about who they were on the inside. The Durples gave them a chance.

"Who-who is that?" yelled Cindyloo, pointing to the sky. They all looked up to see three creatures flying around a big tree.

"Holy kamoli," said Odalee, shielding his eyes from the sun, trying to take a better look. "It flies with its ears! Neato!"

One of the creatures flew up to them and said in a high-pitched, fast, squeaky voice, "We're the Dweeblets and we don't like you. You are different than us and you look funny too!" And they laughed and pointed.

Cindyloo, Mollyboo, Woodroo, Odalee, Princess Lilly, Willy, and Billy all looked at each other in shock.

Mollyboo could see the hurt in her new friend's eyes, and her heart sank. She began to truly understand what her new friends had dealt with their whole lives. Mollyboo turned around with one hand on her hip and the other in the air and yelled, "Don't laugh at us because we're different! We could laugh at you because you're all the same!"

All at once the Dweeblets quit flying and landed on the ground, encircling the Durples.

"We're all unique. We're not the same. We're all differen
no matter what you claim," squeaked one of them.
Mollyboo looked at them with a smirk and said as she
winked at Odalee, "I just judged you by the way that you
look, like you did to us."
The Dweeblets were shocked! Nobody had stood up to
them before, and what this little creature was saying was
so true. They looked at each other with blank expressior
until one finally rhymed, "We're very sorry. You are right.
We shouldn't have judged you for what we saw at first
sight. You will see, if you give us a chance, that we are als
different, than what you saw at first glance."
Odalee started to cry.
"What's the matter?" asked Mollyboo.
"Nothing. These are tears of happiness. This is the most
wonderful moment of my life. I've never had anybody be
this nice to me and then stick up for me. This group of
bullies has just been taught the most important lesson of
all: to not judge anybody by what you see on the outside.
It's what is on the inside that counts. This is a perfect
example! There is a group of us that looks different and

group that looks the same, and each and every one of us
has something special to offer!"
Odalee, Willy, Billy, and Princess Lilly hugged Mollyboo,
Noodroo, and Cindyloo and thanked them over and over
again for giving them a chance. All at once, Odalee played
the mookaluke, and everyone, including the Dweeblets,
sang along.

Let's play the mookaluke,
Let's play the mookaluke,
Let's play the mookaluke, one, two, three.
Don't judge us on what you see,
We're all special and friendly.

After singing and dancing, the Durples, Odalee, Willy, Billy, and Princess Lilly said goodbye to the Dweeblets, who promised they'd never bully again, and continued on their way toward Turpleville.

Would you like to hear a joke? Would you?" asked Voodroo. "How do you catch a unique rabbit? You 'neak up on him!" He laughed uncontrollably. "And how do you catch a tame rabbit? The tame way! Ha, ha, ha!" They all laughed, told jokes, and sang happily as the big oak tree appeared not too far in the distance.

Mollyboo reminded them all, "One day everyone will realize that you have to treat everybody with kindness to make the world a better, more enjoyable place to live in, for everybody. We were all put on this earth for a purpose, and we are all special in a different way."

THE END

Printed in the United States
107992LV00001B